Three Bears
of the
Pacific Northwest

Marcia and
Richard Vaughan

Illustrated by
Jeremiah Trammell

SASQUATCH
BOOKS
SEATTLE

Manufactured in China by C&C Offset Printing Co. Ltd.
    Shenzhen, Guangdong Province, in February 2011
Published by Sasquatch Books
Distributed by PGW/Perseus
17 16 15 14 13 12 11   9 8 7 6 5 4 3 2 1

Cover and interior illustrations: Jeremiah Trammell
Cover design, interior design, and composition: Sarah Plein
Editor: Michelle McCann

Library of Congress Cataloging-in-Publication Data
is available.

ISBN-13: 978-1-57061-684-6
ISBN-10: 1-57061-684-1

Sasquatch Books
119 South Main Street, Suite 400
Seattle, WA 98104
(206) 467-4300
www.sasquatchbooks.com
custserv@sasquatchbooks.com

For Sam "Bear" Vaughan with lots of love. —M.V. & R.V.

Big bear hugs for my parents Helen and Claude Pearson. Special thanks
to Sam and Tracy Cole at Island Adventures, Anacortes, Washington. —M.V.

For Jane Vaughan, a great Mom. And for my friend, Linda Fortune. —R.V.

For my nephew, Thomas "T.P." Phillip. —J.T.

High in the Cascade Mountains, Black Bear was about to cross the road to his favorite berry patch when an RV came cruising around the corner. Suddenly something tumbled out an open window and bounced across the road.

Thump!

Bump!

Thump!

"Ow!" said a little blue teddy bear, rubbing his furry head.

"Are you all right?" asked Black Bear. "What happened?"

"My boy fell asleep and I slipped out of his arms. I have to find him. I'm his favorite toy. He can't sleep without me!"

"Hop on my back," said Black Bear. "I'll help you search."

As they lumbered along, Blue Bear looked at the alpine meadow spotted with wildflowers and the rocky ravines where the last traces of snow hid in the shadows.

"Where are we?" he asked.

"On the mountain where I live," Black Bear answered. "Here's my favorite berry patch. Let's stop for a snack."

"**Yum**," said Blue Bear.
"These purple berries are good!"

After eating their fill, the two bears moved on. As they traveled, Blue Bear saw things he'd never seen before.

"What's that **buzzy** thing on the branch?"

"That's a beehive where I get honey," Black Bear replied.

"What's that hairy thing with horns?"

"That's an elk with antlers."

"What's that black and white striped thing?"
said Blue Bear. "Can I pet it?"

"Look out!" yelled Black Bear. "That's a skunk!"

"**Peeuw!**" shouted Blue Bear.

Holding their noses, the two bears hurried on.

At last the two bears stopped at a stream to drink.

"Where are you going?" asked a curious beaver.

"To find my boy," Blue Bear said.

"Where does he live?"

"In a shiny silver box with wheels," Black Bear said. "But we don't know where to find it."

"My friend Brown Bear is at the bottom of the mountain. She might know. She is very wise," said Beaver. "Just follow this path to the river."

Black Bear and Blue Bear thanked Beaver and took the path through the trees until they came to a racing river.

"Hello," said Brown Bear. "Where are you going?"

"To find my boy," said Blue Bear. "I'm his favorite toy. He can't sleep without me. Can you help us?"

"I'd be happy to. Let's follow the river," said Brown Bear.

So the three bears set off following the
twists and turns of the river until it
spilled into the water that tasted like salt.
Overhead, seagulls circled as a blue heron
waded in the water hunting for fish.

"What kind of bear are you?" Blue Bear asked a spotted creature climbing out of the waves.

"I'm not a bear. I'm a harbor seal. This water is my home. Where is yours?"

"My home is with my boy," said Blue Bear. "We're trying to find it."

"It's a shiny silver box with wheels," said Black Bear.

"Have you seen it?" asked Brown Bear.

Seal shook his head. "No. Maybe it's on the other side of the great water. Follow me and I'll lead you across."

Splash!

Splish!

Sploosh!

The three bears leaped into the water after the seal.

Blue Bear's eyes were wide with wonder as they paddled past ships and boats. Strange creatures swam all around them.

"What's that leggy thing?" Blue Bear asked.

"That's an octopus," said Seal.

"Are those big black and white things sea skunks?"

"No," Seal laughed. "That's a pod of orcas."

"Do they eat teddy bears?"

"No, but they do snack on seals, so let's get going."

They'd nearly reached shore when Blue Bear gasped. "**Wowee!** What's that? It's as big as a house!"

Seal smiled. "That's a gray whale, one of the biggest creatures in the Salish Sea!"

The three bears thanked Seal before climbing to the shore
and continuing on their journey.

Here the forest was dense, damp, and dark. A cool mist floated between tall trees dressed in moss and ferns. The three bears stopped to rest beneath an ancient spruce.

Whoosh. Down swooped a bald eagle. She looked at the travelers with her bright yellow eyes.

"Where are you going?" asked Eagle.

"To find Blue Bear's boy," Brown Bear said.

"Where does he live?"

"In a shiny silver box with wheels,"
Black Bear replied.

"Can you help us look?" asked Blue Bear hopefully.
"We have to hurry. I need to find him before bedtime."

"I can." With a powerful beat of her wings, Eagle snatched Blue Bear up in her talons and lifted him into the sky.

"Whee! I can see so far!" said Blue Bear. "What's that?"

"A waterfall of melting snow," said Eagle.

"Is that a dog with long legs?"

"No," said Eagle. "That's a black-tailed deer."

"What are those steaming pools over there?"

"Hot springs where heated water comes
bubbling out of the earth."

"And that?" asked Blue Bear. He pointed to a
meadow dotted with colorful shapes.

Eagle circled low. "That is a campground
with cars and tents and . . ."

"Shiny silver boxes with wheels!
Is my boy in one of them?"

"Maybe so. But there are too many
people there for me to land."

Eagle circled wide and returned Blue
Bear to his friends.

"We found a campground with shiny silver boxes!"
Blue Bear told his friends. "And I know the way. Come on."

The three bears thanked Eagle and traveled around the
waterfall and past the deer, until they came to a
campground near the hot springs.

"Which silver box is yours?" Brown Bear asked.

"I don't know," said Blue Bear. "But I have to find
my boy soon. The sun is setting!"

On quiet paws they crept along past tents, campfires, and lots
of shiny silver boxes. They peeked inside one RV after
another and saw moms, dads, grandmas, grandpas, and lots
of children. But they did not find what they were looking for.

"Oh, no," sighed Blue Bear as the sun sank like an orange ball behind the Olympic Mountains. "My boy's not here. Maybe I'll never find him. . . ."

As stars filled the sky, Blue Bear heard something that made his ears stand up. It was a familiar cry.

"My boy! Is he in there?" he said, pointing a paw to an RV parked behind a tree. "Let's go see!"

Following the cries, the three bears crept up
to the shiny silver box on wheels.
Blue Bear peeked inside.

"It's him!" Blue Bear shouted. "My boy! We found my boy!"

Brown Bear and Black Bear slipped Blue Bear back into
the arms of his boy. With a squeal of delight, the boy
hugged his teddy bear tight.

Blue Bear waved good-bye to his friends. "Thank you for bringing me home," he said. "And thank you for showing me your world."

"It was our pleasure," Black Bear and Brown Bear said.

And as the moon rose in the sky, all three bears and one happy
little boy settled down for a good night's sleep.

The End